LOST!

LOST!

PATTI TRIMBLE

ILLUSTRATED BY DANIEL MORETON

Green Light Readers
Harcourt, Inc.
San Diego   New York   London

www.harcourt.com

First Green Light Readers edition 2000
Green Light Readers is a registered trademark of Harcourt, Inc.

Library of Congress Cataloging-in-Publication Data
Trimble, Patti.
Lost!/Patti Trimble; illustrated by Daniel Moreton.
—1st Green Light Readers ed.
p. cm.
"Green Light Readers."
Summary: After having been lost in a sink and among unfamiliar objects,
Gil the ant sneaks past a dog and finally finds his way home.
[1. Ants—Fiction.] I. Moreton, Daniel, ill. II. Title.
PZ7.T73525Lo 2000
[E]—dc21   99-50809
ISBN 0-15-202667-3
ISBN 0-15-202634-7 (pb)

A C E G H F D B
A C E G H F D B (pb)

"I'm lost," said Gil the ant.

"Where am I?
It's so wet in here."

"I will walk up," said Gil.

"Now I see.
I was in a sink!"

"What is this?" said Gil.
"It's a big two."

"Oh, it's a clock!"

"Now all I see is pink!" Gil said.
"I will walk on and on."

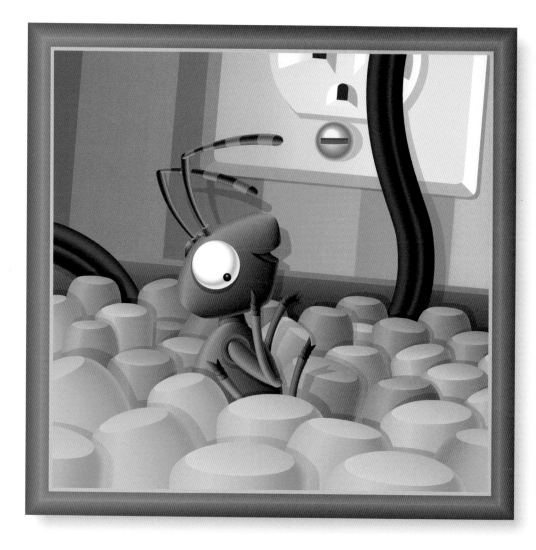

"Oh, it's a pink mat!"

"Help!" called Gil, the lost ant.

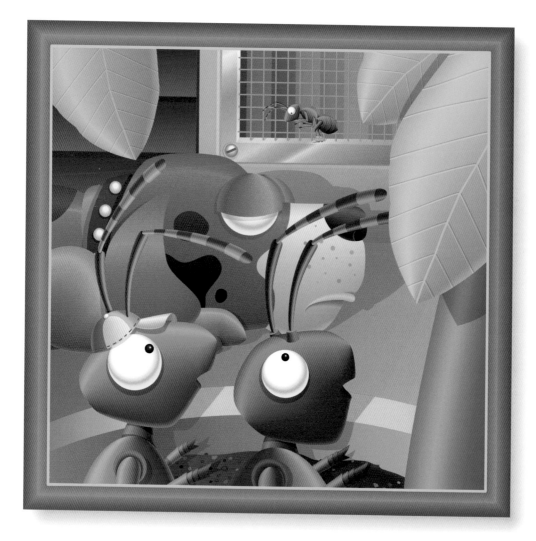

"Sneak past that dog," called his two friends.

"Whew!" said Gil.
"I'm glad to be home!"

Meet the Illustrator

Daniel Moreton loved listening to his grandmother's stories when he was a child. They made him want to write stories and books of his own. He also creates pictures for his books. He uses a computer to draw them, just as he did for this story about Gil the ant. He hopes his stories inspire you to write stories, too!